An Air That Kills

Morgana Somerville

© 2013

An Air That Kills

Honeymead Books

www.honeymeadbooks.com

Published online by Honeymead Books 2013
Copyright © *Morgana Somerville, 2013*

Original Cover Design: Honeymead Books

ISBN 9780992225742

1

I have always been a good girl, I tell myself sometimes. I have always worked hard and looked after Miss Alicia. I have always been there when she needed me. I have always been a clean girl too. I scrubbed up nicely. Master and Missus gave me a generous number of dresses and pinafores and so on, and I have kept them clean and pressed. I washed my face and hands morning and evening, and was allowed a bath once a week – more if I could wangle it, because it has been no holiday being maid to Miss Alicia. All this needs to be said. I know it sounds lowly and common, but it describes how things were. This is a good house, and I like being in service here; and though I would never have ideas above my station I often feel as though Miss Alicia and I were more like friends than mistress and maid. She calls me "Emma", which is my name after all – the rest of the household, not to mention Mister and Missus, calls me by my surname, "Hendry". She lends me her books to read – she lent me *David Copperfield* and *Lorna Doone* and lots of others – though I dare say there would be questions asked if they were found in my little room. We talk about them as I busy myself with my work, and sometimes Miss Alicia stops me and makes me sit down, and we discuss them almost like we're equals.

As I stood behind her earlier this evening, brushing her beautiful, golden hair, I could see that a little frown was furrowing her forehead, as if she was fretting or worrying about something. She certainly was not her usual talkative self, although she often drew in a little breath, as if she were on the point of saying something. I waited patiently. I didn't feel that I could ask to be taken into her confidence – like friends we may be, but I am still only a servant and may not take liberties. After a while she did speak.

"Emma."

"Yes Miss Alicia."

"Just 'Alicia' – this is a time for being frank, and I do not wish for formality. I wish us to be honest with each other," she said.

"Yes, Alicia," I said, hoping that she would be encouraged with just that amount of familiarity.

" Last Sunday the Reverend Kerr preached against women lying with each other as a man lies with a woman," she said, still with a little frown. "Is that what we two do? Do you think that he means the things we do?"

I almost bristled. What a question!

"I'm sure I don't know!" I said. "I have never seen a man lying with a woman! I wouldn't know what they do or how they do it! So how can anything we do be anything like that – whatever it is? Anyhow, we're not women, we're girls."

"You're forgetting that this is to be the evening of my first ball, Emma. Mama keeps telling me that I will consider myself to be a woman from now on."

"Well," I said. "I'm sure Mrs Curtis knows what she is talking about. But myself, well, I would have used the term 'lady' to describe you, or at least what you will be once I get your hair up and get you into that new gown. Anyway, I suppose as such as I don't go to balls at all, then I'm still going to be a girl by the time that you come home – and if Reverend Kerr didn't mention anything about a lady and a girl, then that must be all right!"

"Oh Emma," Miss Alicia laughed, losing the lines of her frown. "You are the wisest person I know – a philosopher, a debater. If John Ridd had been advised by you he could have tangled old Judge Jeffries up in a knot in no time!" She was referring of course to the hero of *Lorna Doone* – I knew that.

We spoke no more about this matter, but now it was my turn to be worried. I am a good girl, and would not like to do anything wrong. I am very devoted to Miss Alicia, in a way I have never been to anyone else; I only want to please her and to make her happy. There can be no doubt that she makes me happy. In her presence, I'm happier than I have ever been. I would never hurt her, or make her do anything wrong. No, decidedly Reverend Kerr is a man of the cloth, almost a gentleman therefore – like Mister and Missus are gentry – and if he says something is so then we have to believe him. I never hear his sermons, because I don't go to St Anne's down in the town, but to little St Mary's chapel down the lane, later on a Sunday with the other servants, and usually a curate comes and takes the service. But if Reverend Kerr has been talking about something being bad, then it can't be our togetherness – mine and Miss Alicia's – because that is all goodness and sweetness!

I helped Miss Alicia to put her hair up. I wish I had golden hair like hers, but I am dark like all our family. I once said as much to her, and she told me not to be silly, and that I was very pretty with my straight, dark hair. I did blush. I always do blush when Miss Alicia says nice things to me. I can't help it. Even when we are very together in our togetherness, even when we are simply "Alicia" and "Emma" and forget that we are mistress and servant, her compliments make me blush. But I must confess it is always a blush of deep pleasure!

With her hair up, I could see her neck, so pale and beautiful. I just gazed at it, longing to kiss it – but this was not the right time for that. But I did catch Miss Alicia's eye in the mirror. She was smiling at me, and that made me feel all right, and I smiled back at her. When she was all dressed – gown, long gloves, fan, a few modest pieces of jewellery – I stepped back to admire her. I had to hold my breath. She was such a lady, such a beautiful lady! No longer the girl I knew, but if I looked I could see that the girl was still there, underneath the lady. It was almost as if she was playing at being a lady, almost a game of dressing up! I felt a lump in my throat, and had to hold back tears; I felt as though the girl I knew was going away, and someone was gradually taking her place – a different person I didn't know.

She lowered her face, then looked up with her eyes. A little smile played on her lips.

"How do I look?" she asked.

"Perfect, Miss," I said. I couldn't say anything more.

Just then we heard someone calling from downstairs.

"Oh!" exclaimed Miss Alicia. "Mama wants me. It must be time to go!"

She darted towards the door, but stopped suddenly and held out both her hands to me. I took them in mine.

"Dearest Emma," she said. "Thank you." I did not really know what she was thanking me for. Was it my help in dressing her, or my advice? Anyhow, she said nothing further, but kissed me lightly on the cheek and hurried out of the room. I listened to her footfalls going down the stairs, and half-heard the urgent conversation between her and Missus, with the occasional baritone of Master adding a burthen to it. I busied myself about straightening her room and getting her nightclothes ready for her return, whenever that might be.

I was, I must admit, very melancholy. In the five years since I came here, despite our difference in station, we had been companions, girls together. Although I was about three weeks older than she was, here I stood still a girl, as far from being a woman as I had been – what? – a year ago. There she was, about to become a lady no less. We were growing apart, it seemed to me.

I could hear hooves and wheels outside, and if I squinted through her bedroom window, I could look down to where the carriage was waiting. I could not resist. I went to the window. There was Master, helping Missus into the carriage. I could see him turn towards the house, and hold out his hand – the gesture was fatherly, adult, but almost a little impatient – then out walked Miss Alicia, and I held my breath. Even from this angle she was the loveliest thing in the whole world. In her new gown, she had taken on an elegance I had not noticed in her before. She had always been straight-backed and poised, but now what I saw was an unaffected composure, an easy confidence. She took her father's hand, used the other to gather the skirt of her gown, and allowed herself to be helped into the carriage. "A princess," I thought. "Just like a princess!" The carriage pulled away. A glimpse of gown through the window, like a patch of sky in a gale. Gone.

"Well, Cinderella," I said aloud. "You shan't go to the ball, so just make the most of it!"

"Is that you, Hendry?" came the voice of Mrs Stephens, the housekeeper, from the landing below. "Stop gibbering and get on with your work!"

"Yes, Mrs Stephens!"

Mrs Stephens was not an unkindly woman, but she didn't stand for wasted breath. I busied myself again. Later, in my room, I had time to sit and think.

As I said, five years ago I arrived here from Shropshire, where I was brought up. My mother had been a lady's maid, as were my two sisters. I was good at my letters and numbers, and would dearly have liked to become a governess or a teacher, but someone of my station did not rise easily to another. So a maid I became, and the household my mum worked for had found me a position here in the Curtis household in Worcestershire. It felt like the other side of the world when I arrived here, not simply a few stations down the railway line, or a boat ride down the river! I had been very nervous, but Master and Missus were kind – they always have been – and Mrs Stephens made allowances, to begin with, for my newness. As for Miss Alicia, she was sunshine, food, and drink to me from the moment I first set eyes upon her. She smiled at me, and chatted away to me as I worked. It was always hard to remember that I had been hired to be her maid, and not her playmate!

I had worked hard to suppress some of my Shropshire dialect – "dunna", and "wunna", and "munna", and the way my voice would go up at the end of a sentence, as if I was asking a question or complaining – but sometimes I would slip into it to entertain Miss Alicia, and she would try to mimic me. It's not easy, it's a subtle way of speaking, and not suited to the voice of someone brought up as gentry. Miss Alicia's voice was always clear – a soprano, the Missus called it – and gentle, regular, sweet. Her laugh was loud, though, if she did not hide it behind her hand. I recall how I had accidentally jammed a drawer back skewed, and the wood grated and squealed.

"Ooh!" I said, with an intake of breath. "He dunna like it, do he!"

How Miss Alica laughed at that. I had said it deliberately, to cover up my clumsiness, and her laughter had been with me, not at me.

"No he dunna, do he!" she replied, and we both laughed. We were allowed to laugh a lot in those days. My role as a playmate as well as a maid was tolerated. In the privacy of her own room, if there was no one else present to whom I had to curtsey and say, "Yes, Ma'am" and "No, Ma'am" to, Miss Alicia and I became very intimate, very intimate indeed I have to say. I would regularly brush her hair, and became used to doing this whilst she was in all states of dress, even that of Eve in Eden. Not that it was ever a commonplace thing; whether in that natural state, or buttoned up in her winter coat and muff, Miss Alicia was never commonplace in my eyes. As she sat at her dressing table, and I brushed her hair over her naked shoulders, I would look at her from head to toe. She knew I looked at her, and she let me admire her; she let me do it without pride, but rather she seemed to appreciate my adoration, and showed her appreciation by giving me the pleasure of seeing her, as an act of generosity.

One day she said, "Kiss me, Emma."

I laid down the brush, and put both hands on her

shoulders. I bent down to kiss her cheek, but at the very last moment she turned her head, and met my lips with hers. I had never in my life felt anything so soft against them. Warm they were too, and sweet. I knew at that moment that I loved her, and I doubted that I could ever love anyone else.

Our first kiss. Neither of us had any idea how a kiss should be, but we pressed our lips gently together, and held them there. It was an awkward pose, with her sitting, and me bending, leaning over her, but I could not tear myself away from her. It was she who broke away, and to me that was like a little death, a little bereavement. But she broke off only to stand up and to walk over to her bed and sit on it, motioning me to come and sit by her. I did so, and as I sat down she put her arm around my shoulders – I put mine round her waist – and we kissed again, closing our eyes. My cheeks were burning, and my heart hammered under my bodice. I felt – I don't know – daring yet afraid. I longed to find out what her bust felt like, but did not know how she would react to being clumsily explored. But my hands were already on her bare skin, weren't they. It would be such a little thing to move one of them. So I stroked her side. She shivered a little, as though I was tickling her. Gradually, I moved my strokes closer and closer towards her chest, until my wrist brushed against one of her nipples. Without taking her lips from mine, she made a little noise, like a lamb bleating several fields away.

I took her little bleat to be a sound of pleasure, and so I boldly cupped my hand round her right breast, feeling her nipple hard against my palm. I gently squeezed, out of curiosity to see how firm it was, and also because it seemed the right thing to do. Alicia put one hand over mine, trapping it against her – as if I had any intention of letting her dear breast go! – stroking my hand to increase the rubbing and squeezing I was giving her. All the time that little lamb-like noise came with her breathing, and all the time. I have no idea how long I held and squeezed her breast like that or kept the contact between our lips, but I do know that it seemed to go on for hours.

Suddenly I realised that she was no longer stroking my hand, but was tugging and pulling at my pinafore, and that she wanted to find a way to my breasts. How clumsy she was, I thought, but then realised that she had been dressed and undressed by me for the past five years, and had very little idea how her own clothes fastened and unfastened, let alone anyone else's. So I let go of her breasts and quickly unfastened my pinafore, the top of my plain dress, and the buttons of my bodice. Like a hungry snake, her hand wriggled inside and began to explore. Her fingers traced back and forth from one nipple to the other, as if comparing them. They tingled under her touch, and I think at that point I too started a little bleat of my own. The touch upon them was like tenderness, almost like soreness, but like a tickle too, and each caress left me wanting another one. I wondered whether that was what she felt when I touched her, so I reached over to her again, and began to rub and chafe at her nipples. The bleating became a purring or a growling in her throat; her eyes were closed tight, and she couldn't hold the kiss steady, pulling slightly away with each outwards breath. Our lips kept meeting in almost a chewing motion, and suddenly that seemed right. We pressed them together again.

I wanted to speak to her. I wanted most of all to say "I love you, Alicia". I wanted to describe how it felt to have her touch me, to be touching her, but words would not form in my mind to match the sensations.

Alicia's hand became indecisive on my breasts. I pushed myself towards it, but it seemed to want to go somewhere else. She slid it down towards my belly, then hesitated. Then, kissing me harder, she seemed to make up her mind, and began to pull up my skirts and to search in my undergarments, finding the nest of curls I – and only I until now – knew was there, and going onward to stroke and stroke and stroke my girlhood.

Breathless minutes passed. Her stroking had made me damp there, and one of her fingers began to slip between its two halves, into the inside tenderness. My heart raced – I felt waves of emotion playing over me, and a delicious sensation in my girlhood. I felt happy and loved, of course, but there was a thrill of wickedness too in letting someone touch me like that. Eventually her stroking found my opening, and gradually, stroke by stroke, she pushed her finger inside me. Each stroke a little further, a little more exciting, a little more wicked – I realised I was moaning softly. Then suddenly there was a sensation inside me as though something had given way – it wasn't sharp enough to be a pain, and it had gone almost as soon as I had felt it. It must have been my hymen, and it must have been in a fragile state in any case, but at least I knew this much, that it had been my lovely Miss Alicia who had taken my virginity!

Miss Alicia now had her finger as far inside me as it would go. As she moved it gently in and out, the palm of her hand rubbed against the top of my girlhood, where a very secret place was! The rubbing was causing me as much pleasure as her finger inside me was, and it was building up.

I realised that she was squirming slightly on the bed, half-pushing herself towards me. I had been letting her do all these things to me, and had not been responding. My hand had become motionless on her breast, merely cupping it. No more – I reached down towards where she was most beautiful, and hastily began to copy what she was doing to me. As my hand touched her girlhood, as my middle finger slipped inside her, she pulled away from our kiss for a moment and gave a great gasp. Inside, she was warm and moist; in fact that moisture seemed to be pouring out over my hand, some of it evaporating into the air as a wild and wonderful scent. I had butterflies in my stomach – no that wasn't it, it was a feeling starting in my girlhood, working its way up through my belly and my chest. My heart was racing, my breathing was shallow.

I have no idea how long it was before the feeling inside me became almost unbearable. For some time Alicia had been pushing her finger inside me in fast bursts, moaning wordlessly as she did so, or seeming to make words that were all "v", or "m", or "n". I had been driven to imitate her finger thrusts, and also I found I was moaning in concert with her. We both seemed to have found a place inside each other so tender, so special, so magical – and yet so basic, like an itch longing to be scratched – and of course there was the pressure we were giving each other on that other secret place…

What happened next was something I could not even describe at the time. Since then I have if not become used to my climax, then certainly I have learned what it is. At that moment in my life it was as startling as falling out of a tree. I remember that once I had been straying in the grounds of the house, where the gardens merge with the nearby forest. Unknown to me the gamekeeper had been just the other side of some undergrowth, aiming his shotgun at a buzzard. When he had let fly, the sound had deafened me, almost knocking me over. Showers of leaves and twigs had fallen around me, I had staggered and swayed, and I think I had screamed as well; certainly for a few minutes I did not know where I was. When Alicia brought me to my first ever climax, that was what it was like. Something like that anyhow.

When I came to, I was sitting on the bed, shaking. My body felt chilled. I looked at Alicia; she had fallen back on the bed. Here eyes were closed but her eyelids were fluttering, and she was panting. I lay down by her, putting an arm round her. We stayed like that for a long time.

That was the first time Alicia and I ever expressed our love in that way. It was not to be the last time. It became part of the rhythm of our lives. I remember thinking, as I lay there with her, that she had no hymen to break. This fact stayed in my mind and worried at me for a long time, until it occurred to me that she rode, and that the exertions of being regularly on horseback could have disposed of it. I am not ignorant. People of my class are not ignorant, though often we are treated as though we're deaf, blind, or invisible.

All the memories of our first lying together came back to me, just as I have recalled them now, as I waited for Miss Alicia to return from her first ball. It was dark when I heard the sound of wheels and hooves outside. I was waiting in the hall to take Miss Alicia's outer clothes and to follow her up to her room. When she entered the house she was subdued, ignored my curtsey, at which she usually smiled, and hurried to her room. As she stood there and I undressed her I noticed a tear on her cheek, but said nothing.

The next Sunday a young man, Mr Alexander Grey, came to spend time with the family.

2

There is a kind of silence which you get in a room when it is empty. You pause at the door, and there is a lightness in the air, which comes from the long stillness of inanimate objects. There may be a small sound – the clock ticking – but that does not break the silence, rather it augments it. There may be sounds outside in the street, or in the garden, or elsewhere in the house; but the room itself is a discrete world, and those extraneous things don't touch it in any way. There is another kind of silence you get when the room is occupied. Maybe the small sound of the clock is there, and nothing else, but the very fact that there is someone, say, standing at the window or seated on a chair, makes the air heavy. Everything is two-dimensional, as though caught in a photograph; but on the other hand, there is a sense that the breaking of the silence is imminent. It may be about to be broken by no more than a sigh or a breath, but broken it will be, and you ache with the tension of waiting.

It was the latter kind of silence which filled the drawing

room, as I stood at the door, and looked in. Madam was sitting in a chair, in the centre of the room. Rather, she was perched on the edge of its seat, absolutely motionless, eyes apparently fixed on the opposite wall. I looked at her face, and for a moment saw Miss Alicia again, but it was only for a moment. Then I noticed she had something in her hand. An envelope, and a piece of paper. A telegram. And then I understood.

I had been 'below stairs', across the scullery yard answering a call of nature, when the doorbell had rung, otherwise I would have answered the front door. Madam had answered it herself, had taken the telegram, and had read it, unprepared. I hesitated for a moment only, and then walked quickly over to her. I knelt by her side, and took hold of the telegram. She wouldn't let go at first, but I pulled gently until it was free of her fingers. I didn't need to read it – in fact I had no right to – but I did. Not that I had any doubt what it would say. "… regret to inform you … Captain Alexander Grey … Killed in action …" or some such wording. It was so.

I put my arm around her waist, and rested my cheek against her shoulder. Neither of us said anything. I was remembering the last afternoon of Mr Alexander's leave, before he returned to Flanders, to his Regiment. Madam was upstairs, and I had gone down into the drawing room to fetch something for her. When I turned to leave, I found Mr Alexander at the door. We stepped aside for each other, and stepped the same way, and then back again, as though we were destined to hinder each other. We both laughed, I with my eyes down, both of us awkwardly and a little shyly. Then we stood opposite each other, as if wondering whether to try another side step.

He had always been a gentle man, not a natural to go for a soldier you would say. He had always treated Madam with great tenderness and kindness, and me with something approaching respect – that surprised me – as if, as a servant, I was in fact a time-served master of a craft, and therefore possessed of a kind of skill that he would never know. It came as a total surprise to me, therefore, when he reached over with one finger, and gently raised my chin, making me look him in the eye. He had never done anything like this before.

"You are a remarkable young woman, Emma," he said.

The look in his eyes was frank and kind – I saw nothing that spoke of lust or force – but this was wrong. That finger seemed to burn on my skin, for all its gentleness; it seemed like something deliberately set out of its place, as though something in an ordered and orderly scene had been misplaced, and was nagging and nagging, just out of reach, begging to be put in it's inch-perfect location.

"We have a saying in Shropshire, Sir," I said, rocking back slightly, so that his finger slid from under my chin. "Why kiss the maid, when you can kiss the mistress."

He stood there, as I pretended to busy myself with straightening something – the imaginary out-of-place thing no doubt.

"Aye, there's the rub!" he said – Shakespeare! I recognised it, and said the name under my breath.

I stopped, and looked him in the eye again, this time of my own free will. I tried to give him a look which was, as his had been, frank and kind. I tried to say something that he would know was kindly meant.

"It's not my business, Sir. I mean that gently – it's not my business."

"No, you're right of course. Thank you for reminding me, Emma. I apologise if I have offended you."

"Not at all, Sir." I curtseyed, and left the room. Now the man to whom I had curtsied was dead, along with so many others of gentle and ordinary birth. By their thousands by now, I supposed. I presumed that my Jack Shaw would soon join that roll call. My Jack Shaw? Jack is Madam's and Sir's driver – madam's only now. He and I are walking out together, and believe me that is all we are doing. I think even Jack is content with things that way, though he did offer to marry me once – the day he enlisted. I was surprised.

"Why, Jack?" I asked.

"I dunno, Emma," he said, his grin broadening his cockney voice. "I think it has something to do with being in love with you!"

"No, no, you idiot – not that! Why did you join up? You of all people!"

How graceless of me to meet a proposal of marriage in that way. But then Jack and I had always laughed like brother and sister, argued like drunks, debated like members of parliament on opposite sides of the despatch box, chatted like friends, and even held hands like children. How could he have expected a conventional answer from me?

"Blimey, girl," he said with mock anger. "I'm blowed if I know why I asked you, if all you can think about is me putting on thc khaki!"

"But Jack," I said, still ignoring the proposal. "You and I have talked this thing over and over – how war is a conspiracy of capitalism, how the working classes shouldn't fight each other, how the only rational course is to refuse to serve, all these arguments you heard at radical meetings. You may not have convinced me entirely, but I can see the point of what the radicals are saying. I thought you believed it too, and would be prepared to stand your ground at a tribunal. And here you are enlisting. You have some explaining to do, Jack Shaw."

Jack set his lip. "I thought it through, Emma," he said. "And I looked deep into myself too. I asked myself if I had the nerve to be a conchie, and the answer I saw inside me was this – maybe yes, maybe no. I asked myself this other question too, could I be a soldier? Could I kill? And the answer I saw inside myself, well, I might not have liked it much, but it was yes. If I saw someone coming for me with a rifle and a bayonet, I could forget that he was just a bloke like me who had the good or bad luck to be born in Germany, I could shoot him without anger or regrct. Shocked myself, girl, but I knew I could do it. It's like it's inside me for a purpose. It's like if I can fight, and I don't fight, then I am trying to be something I ain't. I don't think that it's necessarily right, and I don't think that them that won't fight are necessarily wrong. I could have got the whole thing wrong, but I'm going and that's that. I'm a shilling better off!"

He said all that almost petulantly, but I knew what he meant. And the King could afford to risk a shilling on him. I had been stealing looks at Mr Alexander's books almost as long as I had been in service at his London house, and I had been fascinated by the translations of Socrates and Plato in his bookcase, and the Meditations of Marcus Aurelius. I had not dared to remove any of the books, but I did take such opportunities as I could to read from them whenever time was slack and I could find an excuse to be in the drawing room. So I understood what Jack was saying. There was something inside him which was the nature of what makes a soldier; to have denied it, ignored it, might well have been wrong, cowardly. There was something inside others which made them men of peace, and to deny that would have been cowardly too, though they suffered so for being what they were. Plato would have recognised and honoured both types of men.

This conversation took place, and these thoughts ran through my head, on the embankment by Charing Cross. That was where Jack and I were walking. We walked on for a while, looking at the river, listening to the sounds of London. Then Jack stopped and turned to face me.

"Look here, Emma," he said. "All right so you won't

marry me. I don't mind. We'll just go on as we are. But I want to ask you to do me a great favour. All the soldiers I have ever met carry photographs with them – they'd be of their wives or girls. Will you give me a picture? You're the nearest thing I have to a girl, Emma, even if we aren't going to be married. I can bring the picture out sometimes when I'm away, and seeing you will remind me of all our talks, and of the house, and of ... well ... home. And if anyone asks whose picture it is, I can say it's my girl. There's no harm in saying that is there? It'd only be a white lie."

I couldn't help grinning at this sentimental side of Jack. And yet I felt tears trying to get out. For all his talk of soldicring, he needed something back here to hold onto. I knew enough about his sensitivity to know that he had doubts, and fears. To my mind, doing something you feel you must despite doubts and fears – that's what makes a hero. I would not refuse this hero that one simple request.

"Of course you can have my picture, Jack. And you can tell them what you like about me. I'll be too far away to care what they think! And you can write to me too, and if you really want to put 'Sweetheart' or 'Darling' in the letter, you do that. What's a few more white lies now we've told one!"

We stood and looked at each other for a while, and then he sighed.

"Emma, I'm sorry to say I think you will die an old maid."

"I hope so, Jack. The older the better. I would hate to go before my time!"

We laughed. That was as close as I had ever come to marriage, and at least Jack Shaw had had the decency to ask me in his own right. When I looked back at the way Miss Alicia had been courted by Mr Alexander – for all his gentleness, it was as though he had made a business agreement with the Curtis family, as though a contract had been signed for the delivery of Miss Alicia on some future date, delivery to be made at St Anne's church on the so-and-so day of such-and-such month in the year of Our Lord something-or-other. They had met on the evening of her first ball, that day when I had dressed a girl who came home a lady. Their courtship had, as far as I could judge, been very formal. The important thing seemed to have been that Mr Alexander had met with the approval of the Curtis family from the very beginning. I had the impression that Miss Alicia felt that she was obliged to marry him. My childhood companion had become more and more distant from me, more and more withdrawn, even calling me "Hendry" rather than Emma. Her smiles became more infrequent, rather like something she wore on special occasions; more than once I caught her doffing her long, solemn face before she came round a corner or through a doorway, and donning the smile which everyone expected.

On the fewer and fewer occasions when she took me in her arms, I had felt a kind of desperation, and when we lay together on the night before her wedding, the gentle climax I gave her was followed by tears.

I had not been at the wedding, of course. I had been waiting at the house to help Miss Alicia change from her wedding dress into her going-away clothes after the wedding breakfast. And of course I had dressed her in that wonderful garment. I couldn't help but thinking of her as a mayfly, dancing on white wings for a single summer day, then never to be seen again – the cruellest jest of nature. For that is what a beautiful bride must be, simply a thing of wonder for the day of that one great show she puts on. Then she is gone. Or she has passed out of our sight and has become something else. Bride is a once-only word; wife is a lifetime notion. Did Miss Alicia look beautiful as a bride? She could not have looked more beautiful if she had stepped naked from a sea-shell! As though one could ever paint a lovely lily, but oh this lily looked so much more than lovely. When it came time for her to go down from her room to the hall, and out to the waiting carriage, she moved through the house like a shaft of brilliant sunlight through rapidly-moving cloud. I followed her with my eyes. How I loved her!

And now here we both were, back as we had been before. Neither of us had a husband, and yet we were not as we had been before. The things we had lived through in the few short years since our first kiss admitted of no going back. She was still Alicia, but was also Madam; I was still Emma, but was principally Hendry. Around us the world seemed to be going

33

mad, but maybe we were the mad ones, drawing in the walls of the London house around us. On the day that the telegram arrived, once I had prized it from her fingers, I took her gently upstairs and got her to lie down on her bed. I fetched a blanket and spread it over her, then stood and watched her motionless figure. After a while I crawled under the blanket and held her close to me. We lay there for several hours in a room full of silence. Even the loss of a husband whom you can never bring yourself to kiss is still a loss. I could give her my arms to lie in, and I knew I would do so again and again. I would be myself, she would be herself, and if she needed me I would be there. But the silence persisted; it needed a sob to break it but a sob never came. It was as though the world held its breath. Would she ever cry for him?

For now, all I could do was listen to the silence in her room, and be part of it.

3

"They have left you all on your own!"

I looked up from the book I was reading. She was standing with the sun behind her, but I could make out that it was Mrs Patel. The slight figure in her wrapped Indian dress – a *sari*, she called it – was unmistakable. Her voice was soft and gentle, a tinkling soprano, and it left one in no doubt that her face, despite being in shadow, had a smile on it. Mine did not – I believe I had forgotten how to smile.

"Yes, they've left me on my own. But I don't mind. Really I don't."

"Oh but you do, Miss Hendry," she said, sitting on the grass beside me, folding her legs underneath her in one graceful movement. "Forgive me, Miss Hendry, but you do mind such a lot. I can see it in your face. May I call you Emma?"

"Yes," I said. I supposed that this was an intrusion, and had almost made up my mind to insist on my privacy, when I suddenly realised several things. Firstly, this privacy of mine, which I had enjoyed for most of the time since I had come to the island, was in fact a painful, lonely, purgatory, into which I had been dumped, whether I willed or no, by Mrs Grey – Alicia – and those beings I called, in my own mind, 'her dramatic women'. Secondly, Mrs Patel's intrusion was the first thing that had broken the chains of the tedium of that privacy, and I was glad of her company. Thirdly, I could tell that she was kind, guile-less, and curiously child-like. Her approach was open and honest.

"You may call me Draupadi," she said, and then giggled, clumsily hiding her laughter behind her hand, but revealing a dazzling, gat-toothed smile. She looked at me over her round spectacles.

"Why are you laughing?" I asked.

"My name," she said. "I couldn't expect you to understand the reference. It is from an old Indian story – the

Mahabharath – there was a character, a beautiful maiden. 'Doe-eyed Draupadi' she was called. My parents named me after her, thinking that they would have a beauty for a daughter. Well, I hide my doe-eyes behind spectacles. Without them I am myopic, and peer about me like some creature of the dark!"

"It's a beautiful name," I said. I almost went on into goodness-knows-where-land, but instead we suffered a few seconds' uncomfortable pause. "Teach me how to say it properly."

"Drau-Pa-Di," she enunciated, and I copied it a few times. It felt exotic on my tongue, like a new taste, and I wanted to keep on saying it. I didn't, though. I stopped after a few times, and hid it away for future pleasure. The instant ease of her company, the instant familiarity of her approach, her relaxed conversation – all of this was a new, unexpected, awakened pleasure.

Suddenly she stood up again, and held out her hand to me.

"Come with me. There is something I want to show you."

I got up, and took her hand. It was soft, warm, slender, and instantly gripped mine as tightly as a young playmate's might. She half turned, and began to step away, pulling me with her. We walked hand-in-hand over the spare grass, through a small, half-neglected orchard of olive-trees which stood by the villa, and out into the countryside. Uphill we went, and followed a narrow path. She went ahead, twisting her arm behind her, never letting go of my hand, guiding me along, pace after steady pace. I followed her, almost meekly, certainly with an absolute trust which surprised me. The feel of her hand in mine gave rise to a frisson – or was that the perspiration between my shoulder blades reacting to the breeze which now rose from the sea, as we climbed higher and higher. We said nothing to each other, until she paused for a moment, and turned her gaze to a fold in the landscape, through which sand and sea were visible.

"Look," she said, pointing, and I recognised the cove into which I had first sailed, a week or more before. I recalled standing rather unsteadily, holding my hat on my head, on the deck of the little fishing boat which had ferried us from our steamer. How had I come to be here?

Madam – Mrs Grey – my Alicia – had surprised me one day by saying: "No one has a maid these days. You shall be my companion instead. When we go travelling, you shall be my travelling companion. There is no need to call me Madam any more. In public I shall be Mrs Grey, and in private you may call me Alicia. We have known each other long enough."

There had been no "if that is all right with you" or anything, but then she had never, in all our years together, found the right level on which we could deal with each other. Only in love-making had we been equals, only in these often tender, sometimes clumsy, occasionally ecstatic times had we been simply two people. Only then had we truly loved each other, truly been as comfortable as we were as children. I regarded her more recent decisions and attitudes to be due to her 'dramatic women'.

These influences would come into the house on gusts of

outdoor air – all black clothes, flowing scarves of batik, large hats, long cigarette-holders, loud voices full of opinion and strident philosophy. Had any of them actually worn stockings then I suppose one could have called them 'blue-stockings', but flapping, black coolee-trousers seemed to be de rigueur amongst them. They pontificated loudly on art, politics, literature, free love, Jazz and Stravinsky, the proletariat, vegetarianism. Mrs Grey filled her bucket at their well, and drank as deeply as she dared, flirting more with the coolee-trousers and the cigarette-holders than with the 'dramatic women', but returning more often than not to the skirts in which she was comfortable (and in which I, if no one else, preferred to see her). As I said, she flirted with their ideas most of all, not so much with them, but I still had to be mute if I saw one of them drape an arm around her shoulders, or openly kiss her long and deep, or take her off goodness-knows-where for a couple of hours or a night. I know I was jealous, but mostly I saw all this as being a violation of her, an exploitation of her, rather than an usurpation of my tenuous place in her heart and in her bed. I suspected them of being interested in her money. Her brothers, as well as Captain Grey, had died in the Great War, and she now had her parents estate – I never heard that any of the dramatic women worked, or had incomes, but they came and went as house-guests, seldom returning the hospitality.

Mrs Grey had announced one day that we were all to travel to the Mediterranean, and would take a steamer around the Greek Islands. One of the dramatic women had secured a villa. It was after this announcement that she declared me no longer to be her maid. I had no doubt, however, that companionship would be no more than a part of my duties, and that I would continue as maid in all but name. I had no doubt either about who would be paying for the jaunt.

We two had been the last of our party to leave the steamer – not least because Mrs Grey had nervously packed, un-packed, and re-packed her valise and trunk, and had fretted as they were lowered into the fishing boat. Mine had been packed for hours, and had in fact been taken off with the luggage belonging to one or more of the dramatic women; I found it later, abandoned in the kitchen of the villa.

The cruise in the steamer had given me my sea-legs, but

the little boat had dived and bobbed in the swell. As we entered the cove where we were to land, I believe it had been bravado on Mrs Grey's part, to counter her nervousness at the yawing of the boat, which had led her to declaim an introduction to the island. She had swept her arm out, half turning to me.

"This is Lesbos," she had said. "This is where Sappho…" Her voice trailed off.

"I know," had been my simple reply. "I have read her poetry, such as has been found."

"You never cease to surprise me, Emma my dear!" had been her only comment. Oh Alicia – if only you had taken more time away from the dramatic women, I would have been less of a surprise to you…

There they had all stood, in various poses on the beach. My eye had only half taken in the small figure I later knew as Mrs Patel. Later that day, as evening fell, she had sung to us, in a small but metallically clear soprano. Folk songs in Hindi and Gujarati, ancient songs of devotion in Sanskrit. It had been as though they had brought a tame canary to amuse them, and they had applauded, with cries of "Delightful, darling!", and then went back to their discussions – the wheel of life, karma, Ahimsa, the origins of Indo-European language, the scientific enquiries of the ancient Ionians, the march of civilisation from Mahenjo-Daro through Mesopotamia to Europe – while Mrs Patel had sat, serene and calm as a statue of a Bodhisattva, sipping her tea.

Now she was here with me, no longer 'Mrs Patel' but Draupadi, on a smooth promontory, above my arrival-cove. There was a breeze here, but a natural dip in the ground gave some shelter from it, and the sun was warm. Draupadi's firm hand pulled me the few steps into this natural bowl. I looked around, and saw that our horizon was the lip of bowl, only a few feet away. We were above everything, but unseen.

"How did you find this hide-away?" I asked. Draupadi said nothing, but when I turned back to her, I found that she had stepped out of her sandals, had laid her spectacles safely inside one of them, and was unwinding and folding her sari. Her movements were both graceful and unaffected, and held

43

my attention, so that it hardly registered with me that she was naked. When at last I did gaze at her body, I realised how perfect she was. Her skin was a uniform brown all over, almost [it struck me] the colour of the olives in the orchard through which we had passed on our way up here. She was slender, but her limbs were rounded, and in exact proportion to her body. Her hips were round, yet she was not pear-shaped, and though she was smaller than me, she held her back and shoulders straight, and that gave her a tallness that was of bearing rather than height. She seemed to be a princess – a *Rani* – as if she had stepped out of the very legend from which her name had come. She was smiling. Her eyes were an honest chestnut, and indeed I thought suddenly that they were indeed the eyes of a doc. But their charm was not that of a shy animal, because there was laughter in them, and her smile broke now and then into half a grin, revealing her teeth. She was not self-conscious, except perhaps for those teeth. They were level and white, but had pronounced gaps between them – maybe she thought this was not a good feature, but I thought they made her. With supposedly perfect teeth she would have been, well, like a meal without seasoning.

She stepped up to me, put her arms around my neck, and kissed me. Her kiss was gentle and tender, yet it lingered insistently. Her breath was sweet – I had expected it to be hot, like Indian cooking.

"You are very beautiful," I said, when her lips left mine.

"I have been told that." There was no vanity in her reply.

"It's true." We kissed again, and I pulled her to me, feeling the softness of her back with my hands. She took one hand from round my neck, crooked her arm between us, and slipped that hand into my blouse, and beneath my camisole. That hand formed a cup around my right breast, and my nipple lodged between her fingers, as she gently stroked me. For a moment I thought, "I am being unfaithful to Alicia!" But the next thought was, "So what? She is always unfaithful to me!" That thought was more shameful to me than the first, but close behind it came another one, which comforted me again. "No, this is something different. This is me and Draupadi."

"I have never been undressed by anyone," I said. "Would

you undress me?"

Draupadi stepped back a little, smiling, always smiling, and began to unbutton my blouse. It slipped down over my shoulders and fell to the ground. She lifted my arms above my head, and then pulled up my camisole free of my reach. For the first time in my life, my breasts were bare in the open air. I almost covered them shyly with my arms, as if ashamed, but encouraged by Draupadi's smile, I held my arms loosely by my side. I expected her to unfasten my skirt, but instead, with her smile becoming cheeky, she bent and reached her hands up inside it, and tugged down my bloomers, making me feel somehow deliciously sluttish. I stepped out of them, knowing that I was naked underneath my skirt now. Only after stepping back and looking at me for a while, did she step up to me once more, finally to unfasten my skirt. I let it drop to the ground. I was as naked as she was.

She stepped up to me and kissed me again – oh so sweetly. To me it did not seem to matter that she must have been with other women before; she was a creature out of legend, stepping from the pages of a centuries-old Hindu tale of gods and battles and beautiful doe-eyed maidens. She had been created for this very moment, brought to be part of my karma, my life-story, my destiny. She had been fashioned to love me, for eternity or for an instant.

Bending down she began to lick around my left nipple, saturating it with her saliva, blowing on it from a few inches away to make it feel cold. Taking some saliva from her tongue onto the fingers of her left hand, she darted it down quickly to touch my womanhood. But she didn't linger for long there, collecting more moisture on her hand from my seeping spring, and moving her hand away as though the whole thing had been a mistake or a tease. But she then coated her own left nipple with this mixture, making it glisten in the sunlight. I looked in amazement, knowing that what was shining there on her beautiful breast was mostly my product. Cupping both hands under her breasts, she pressed against me, kissing me again. She rubbed her breasts against mine so that dry nipple met wet, and wet met dry, sliding over each other, until each was equally sticky with a wonderful traction. I had never felt anything like this in my entire life. Draupadi seemed to speak a different language with her whole body than the barebones-

Saxon that Alicia and I used for our sexual conversations!

Draupadi was all caressing hands, soft, musical speech that I could not understand, pressing warmth, utter love expressed physically. I have little idea how we came to be lying down, crooked head-to-womanhood like a figure six and a figure nine. But here we were. I knew that her tongue was upon my clitoris, and absurdly my mind was tracing the Greek etymology of the word, as if I was trying to distract myself from the build-up of sensation and emotion. Mine was on hers, tasting her, teasing down a steady rain-shower of her juices to soak my face. She had fingers inside me – two? three? I could not tell – and had found my sanctum sanctorum; I was striving for hers. To my shock, she had gently slid one juice-soaked finger inside my back passage, and was teaching me how to love, with relaxed muscles, that gentle in-and-out stroking; I followed suit. When climaxes did break over us, like the salty waves of the Aegean, my cry of ecstasy was almost one of pain or despair, whilst hers was like a little song, the trilling of a lark. Then, there, in that transient moment, I loved her and she loved me, and we were complete.

I remember little of dressing, nor of walking hand-in-hand back to the villa. I was happy for the first time in my life. I had been taught about love by an equal, and it was a magical thing. I would never be the same again. If I never made love again in my whole life, then this beautiful, holy unfaithfulness would forever hang like an icon before my eyes.

Alicia and her dramatic women arrived back from their trip, hot and loud-mouthed, demanding drinks and dinner. Drinks came, dinner came, drinks and dinner went. Discussion followed, and then someone called upon Mrs Patel to sing.

Draupadi stood and, as was her wont on these occasions, moved to the outside of our circle, to stand behind one of us. She chose me, and stood with one gentle hand on my shoulder. She announced a folk song – a story of love between a village boy and girl – and sang it, a clear and simple tune in a cheerful key or mode, which held the attention of all except perhaps the two most Philistine of the dramatic women, and even they were shamed into silence and had to listen. At the end there was applause, and she bent to whisper in my ear.

"I changed the words from boy and girl to girl and girl. And I managed to make one name sound like 'Emma'."

My face burned. I felt as though I had been made love to again.

Two days later, for whatever reason, Alicia had decided that she and I were leaving. The other dramatic women would stay there until the summer lease on the villa had run out. It the hustle-bustle of re-packing our luggage, I had little time to think about the doe-eyed Mrs Patel – my Draupadi – until the morning of our departure. She came to me at one of the rare moments when I was alone with the baggage, and stood in front of me. I wanted to speak to her at length, but she put one finger to my lips to silence me.

"For me," she said. "Don't be sad. Forget nothing, regret nothing."

I nodded, but I knew that though her advice was wisdom distilled, I would find it impossible to follow. And so when, later that day, our little boat sailed briskly out of the cove, I kept my eyes upon the still figure in the bright sari.

Even when I could make out nothing I kept looking at the island. And when we had transferred to the steamer, I stood at the rail, watching Lesbos become a smudge upon the horizon, and then merge with the sky. Then I kept on standing there for no reason at all, until I became very cold.

4

For the second time in my life, the world has gone completely mad. If I try to do anything and I find it's forbidden, or I grumble about being forbidden to do it, as sure as dried eggs are bloody dried eggs someone will say, "Don't you know there's a war on?" What a fatuous question! There are sandbags on the street, air-raid sirens going off, blackout curtains, and God knows what else to remind us that there is indeed a war on. Marching feet are nothing but an echo in the mind now, which reverberates whenever one contemplates a street populated by only women and the elderly.

Long ago – or so it seems – Alicia's dramatic women faded away at the same rate that her beauty did. The austerity of wartime, the rationing of food, the coarseness of the fabric of our clothes all chipped away at the remaining strength of her mind. It was never very strong in the first place. Her body has followed, so that now - grey-haired, sere, gaunt, near-blind, near-demented – she has the appearance of someone ten, twenty years beyond her age. My heart has been close to breaking for so long now that I cannot remember it ever being whole. But it does not break, it holds, I hold. For Alicia.

The same things that have hurt her seem to have rallied me. The diet of rationed food and the PT lessons at the Fire Station have trimmed my figure. The cut of my jacket, and the need to balance a metal helmet on my head have given an extra straightness to my bearing, with the result that my bust is high on my ribcage. Ten years seem to have fallen from me, and the gulf between myself and Alicia has sometimes seemed too great to span. My ill-temperedness at folk who remind me that there is a "war on" is something which keeps me going, and for all the hate I feel for this mad world, when I stop and think about it, I smile a lot. I smile, that is, when I forget to stop and think, which is mercifully often. I smile behind the desk where I typewrite for Britain, when I consider the gallantry of the volunteer firemen at the station. Many of them are conscientious objectors. Outside the station they suffer taunts, showers of spittle, and blows from people who think they're cowards for not being in the army. They take all this patiently, never raising a hand in retaliation. When I step in to defend them it's a case of "You stay out of this, Miss – it's not your business!" As if once, long ago, I did not have someone who came back from a war half the man he had been, a dear friend who had seen friends killed and had killed foemen, and who had come back bitter, utterly convinced of the wrongness of it all.

Jack Shaw had never returned to the London house, where we still lived. Alicia and I travelled everywhere by taxi, except when I went out alone and I used the omnibus. It was on the top deck of a bus in Oxford Street, one day in the middle of the Depression, that I recognised a man hunched in a raincoat. Even from the back, even years later I would have recognised him. My Jack Shaw. The eyes that greeted mine were, however, hard and shifty; they had lost the trust and openness that they once had. We conversed – I even told him to look me up at the house, though God knows why – but he seemed to be a shell, or to have been emptied of what was there when I walked out with him and filled with something else. A demonic possession, but the demon was a banal and petty demon. He wouldn't talk of the Great War as such, but when I egged him on to rediscover some of his past idealism he shook his head.

"I've seen things, Emma. It's an ugly world. I may have stuck it out, but I have seen men ripped apart, shattered. The lucky ones were the ones whose bodies were killed, the unlucky ones were the ones whose minds were killed. Sometimes I think I'm one of those, but I seem too sane to be. But I tell you this, Emma – it's all shit, all of this," This was the only point at which he took a hand out of his raincoat pocket; he waved violently at the London scene through which we were passing. I could see that there was something wrong with that hand, I caught a fleeting glimpse of scar tissue as if he had been burned; but he shoved it back into his pocket too quickly for me to see much. For the same moment as he gave the wild gesture, the hardness of his eye turned to a blazing coal, but it was unpleasant to see, hateful … and hate-filled.

Eventually we reached his stop, and I watched him stride down the street, still hunched, still with his hands thrust deep into his pockets, only occasionally giving a look to left or right. I never saw him again, but I did hear that he was sent to prison for some petty crime.

I have seen the evil spirit that dwelt in him at work here

during this new war. It is abroad, it is everywhere, it inhabits the people who spit at the firemen, the ambulance drivers, the people who volunteer to have new medicines tested on them, any man not in uniform. It is there in the wicked glare of women who shun a woman because she can't stand her loneliness, and has more than her share of visitors. It is just there. The shattered minds, the borderline insanity, the tight-rope that is walked on the edge of cracking, I have seen all that. Oh make no mistake, if we come through this and write our own history, then what we will boast of will be the pluck, the helping hands, the cups of tea handed round, the dogged spirit of our city folk. But we are tired, and the only people who thrive are the stupid and the cunning, those who seem to slip scot-free past the conscription and past the hatred of the small-minded, because they wield an arcane, underground influence over everyday folk. If Hitler walked in tomorrow, those people would gladly work for him, and the rest of us would be too tired to do anything but hail him as a liberator, freeing us from all of life's problems.

Do you want to know what I see? I walk home at night, and I walk quickly; but I see the beatings-up, the wallet-

An Air That Kills

snatching, the back-alley sex. I have seen murder, and have passed by on the other side, just like anybody else. None of us will get involved, not even most of the bobbies. Jack Shaw's words come back to me time and time again. God forgive me, I feel like sweeping my hand out in his dismissive gesture and consigning us all to hell. I don't know if we would notice the difference. The imps stoking out fires would look exactly like the cunning and the stupid who are thriving here on the hard streets of London.

Let me tell you, I am exhausted. As I stand here with my key in my hand, ready to enter the house once more, I no longer know whether my lean fitness is enough to take me through another night. Suddenly I have had enough.

As I walked home tonight, I think the baleful spirit of the age almost got me too. My aloofness almost cracked. And the funny thing was that this had absolutely nothing to do with the evening's events. I think that I was resolutely counting my steps home, deliberately putting one foot in front of the other in an attempt to stay sane, as if the ordinariness of the movement was in itself a formula for warding off madness. I was only vaguely aware of other footsteps in the street, and when a man fell in step with me I didn't feel any surprise, just puzzlement. There was nothing unfriendly or suspicious about him. He tipped his hat, he kept at arm's length.

"You look lost, Miss. Do you need seeing somewhere?" he said, and his voice sounded friendly.

Absurd, though – of course I was not lost, I lived here. But suddenly yes, I was gripped by something and the familiarity of the streets faded. I was in a landscape of shadow, with only my flashlight and his making any penetration. Where was I? Had I in fact taken a wrong turn in my stupor? I muttered something, hardly raised my eyes, and allowed him to keep pace with me. I told him where I was heading.

"Oh that is on my way," he said. "I'll see you there."

He kept up his friendly banter, and I replied monosyllabically. I seemed to be only half-aware of him as we walked along. I don't even think I woke up from this dream-walk on the edge of sanity when, as we passed the mouth of a dark alley, he shoulder-charged me into it, seized me, and bore me against a wall.

"Now don't you make a sound, Miss." More and more absurd, that he should keep calling me "Miss" now. As he pushed his face next to mine, and thrust his hands inside my jacket, I recognised him – the spirit of the age had come to me in the flesh. Make a sound? I was struck dumb, paralysed, couldn't get my breath. I opened my mouth and no sound came out. I thought of struggling but somehow the will to resist was not there. When he began to pull at my uniform trousers, when he said, "I'll bet your cunt is gorgeous – I'm going to fuck you…" all my brain could do was take in his accent, finding it ridiculous to hear the London twang, almost forcing me to laugh at "fack" and "kant". Maybe it was the last ditch stand of my sanity, but as he violated me I kept going over something in my mind…

"Kant. Immanuel Kant, born in Konigsberg in 1724, died in 1804. His central thesis…" I had actually read about this "… that the possibility of human knowledge presupposes the active participation of the human mind, is deceptively simple, but the details of its application are notoriously complex...." I went over and over all I knew about this philosopher, remembering a list of his books, while what was happening to me happened as I stood there and passively let it happen. The part of my mind which was not detached was the part which shocked me. I was being degraded, but there was an aspect of this that seemed to thrill me, to say yes, at last the spirit of the age is here, has defeated me, why bother, I am trash! That part of me gave in to the degradation almost willingly.

When at last he pushed me aside, grabbed my handbag, and ran, I stood there for – what? – minutes I supposed, still mesmerized partly by the casual brutality and by my complicity, as it felt to me, and partly by the stream of thoughts about Immanuel Kant which kept on circulating in my mind. Almost casually I rearranged my clothing and stepped out onto the street. As if a mist had cleared, as if the brutality had forced my eyes open, I now recognized where I was, and started to walk to the house. It was only two minutes away from where I had been attacked, two minutes from where I had capitulated, two minutes away from where I had let the aggressor march in and claim that he had liberated me. As I walked on, I felt no fear; after all, the spirit of the age had just claimed me – what else could possibly happen to me now?

So here I am, entering the house, carefully closing the door behind me before switching on a light. From upstairs comes Alicia's querulous call, "Is that you?" She never says "Is that you Emma?" or even "Hendry", so in truth anyone who enters the house could answer truthfully "Yes"! I call back to her.

"Yes dear, I'm back. Sorry I'm a little late. I lost my…"

What did I lose? I was possessed by the spirit of the age, that was for sure. Maybe it was my sanity I lost. Maybe that's it – I am mad, and that is why I can cope with it all. I take my jacket off, hang it on the coat-stand, noticing that a couple of buttons are torn loose and for a moment wondering how that happened. Then I remember, of course, Immanuel Kant did it, the spirit of the age, and I almost laugh. I climb the stairs.

There is nothing wrong with Alicia's hearing, but she calls, "Speak up, dear. You lost something. What did you lose?"

"My handbag," I say.

"Well that is very careless of you."

Yes, it was very careless of me to lose my handbag like that, and possibly my sanity too. I walk into Alicia's bedroom. She has retired to bed early – not that she spent much time actually on her feet today. I sit on the edge of the bed and allow her to grab hold of my hand. Her thin fingers bring a shock of pity to my heart.

"Shall I make you some supper?" I ask. "A warm drink?"

"No, nothing. Thank you. How was your … your … where it is you go to?"

"Fine."

"You came safely home?"

Well I am here so I nod. What could I tell her? I met Immanuel Kant but he has been dead since 1804, so it must have been a spirit I met? I have lost my mind? I have let the liberator march in? I have capitulated? A noise begins to fill my head, and I shake it to try and kill it, but it won't go away. Only gradually do I realise that the noise is not inside my head. It is a siren, several sirens – there is an air-raid. Soon the sirens are joined by distant thuds, as bombs fall somewhere across town. Alicia is gripping my hand and shaking it like an otter shaking a fish.

"I won't go to the cellar – don't make me, please don't make me!" she is saying.

"Shush, shush, we'll stay here if that's what you want." Perhaps my life is charmed now, anyway, being a child of the spirit of the age. Alicia, for some reason is afraid of the cellar. I used to be too.

The bombs begin to fall closer now. We can hear the faint scream of their descent, and each thud, growing nearer, becomes a crash, with an after-sound of falling masonry. What must be a whole bomber-load is falling no more than two streets away, making its wicked obliteration under cover of darkness; when daylight comes eventually the memory of what was standing where rubble remains, will be weak and watery. The ground beneath the house convulses with every approaching explosion, shaking the furniture, causing little snowfalls of loose plaster from the ceiling. The last crash, in the next street causes the light in our landing and in Alicia's room to flicker out. Alicia gives a shrill little cry, and throws herself into my arms, clinging onto me in the dark.

"There, there," I say. "We'll be all right. They missed us."

Then another load begins to descend, and in my mind I can picture them eating away at the houses in our street. The scream of the falling bombs becomes terrifyingly loud. Alicia, shivering in my arms, suddenly feels like the girl I knew all those years ago, she of the fair skin and hair, of the beautiful deportment, the love of my early years with whom I had shared Blackmore, Dickens, Austen, Shakespeare … everything.

A deafening scream and crash – was that the house next door? Suddenly Alicia surprises me with a passable attempt at the Shropshire dialect I had tried to teach her in those days.

"Ooh – he dunna like it, do he?"

"No, he dunna, do he!" I reply.

"Darling," says Alicia. "Say a prayer. Please."

Prayers? I don't think I know any. If I do they have been knocked out of my head tonight. From somewhere I dredge up a piece of poetry – the only thing that comes to my mind. Houseman. "A Shropshire Lad"

Into my heart an air that kill
From yon far country blows:
What are those blue remembered hills,
What spires, what farms are those?
That is the land of lost content,
I see it shining plain,
The happy highways where I went

And cannot come again…

"Amen," says Alicia, content that I have said something.

An air that kills. The killing air is screaming now. Directly over our heads. Screaming with that fell descent, the true spirit of the age, of which he whom I met tonight is just the idiot, bastard son. As I lie here with Alicia in my arms, holding close to me the only person I have ever truly loved – this frightened thing, this broken, lovely thing, now smelling again of freshness and youth, as dear to me as anything – at last I understand. I remember our speaking, all those years ago, about the Reverend Kerr preaching against two women lying together as a man and a woman would. Well tonight I felt I had learned the difference, first by my encounter with "Kant" the idiot, bastard son of the spirit of the age, and now with my little Alicia lying in my arms. There was no comparison, there is no comparison, and that truth is setting my mind free at last. Tonight, I reflect with a wry grin that would dazzle you if there was any light here, I will have lost my virginity, my handbag, and my life! How funny that is. And I don't think I mind any more, even though I am scrambling through my memories trying to recall the sweetest, the things I might regret losing in a final moment. Even though I am wondering why my life does not, as I think it ought by right, to flash through my mind. No blue remembered hills, even, from my childhood. Wait – one face, that of Draupadi, smiling, saying with gentleness, "Forget nothing, regret nothing." Then she fades, and now I do feel mocked because I can truly remember nothing as the image of young Alicia fades too, and the words of Reverend Kerr – what were they? What was it all? Where is the understanding of a moment ago?

And the air that kills is closer. Its scream is deafening, painful, too painful to bear, as is life at this last moment, as are the forgotten happy and unhappy highways where I cannot come again. The sole consolation I have is this: very soon, any instant now, it will stop. Everything will stop.

An Air That Kills

www.ingramcontent.com/pod-product-compliance
Lightning Source LLC
Chambersburg PA
CBHW061138200626
46817CB00016B/2058